SS 2/23

MW01139661

THE GOOD SHEPHERDS

A Short Christmas Story by Michael F. Tuman

Please visit the Authors Blog at:
flyingmonkey5november.com
Other works by Michael F Tuman
UNJUSTIFIED MANIA
A Novel of Police
THE PUBLIC GUARDIANS
A Dark Comedy

FORWARD

While working the Midnight shift 12AM until 8AM as a police officer in Chicago on Christmas eve I would often fancy myself one of the shepherds watching over the flocks, of citizens. Aside from the dispatchers breaking the radio silence with their possible sightings of Santa Clause things were usually quiet. I had the same feelings when I was deployed overseas.

One of my most vivid recollections of the Army was in Haiti Christmas 1994. I was standing on the back of a HMMWV Humvee, Hummer singing Christmas carols with the local children of Les Cayes. They knew all the words to "Angels We Have Heard On High", "Les Anges dans Nos Campagnes" in French. That Christmas Eve, surrounded by the children, I felt a power in the air. Again, I felt like a shepherd watching over the flocks.

So, as a kid I wanted to fight evil. I wanted to be some sort of super hero. I wanted to be a leader and protector. I had the pleasure of being better than any superhero. I was a soldier and police officer. Being a Soldier gave me the opportunity to be a leader and being a Police officer allowed me to protect. Neither profession is on the celebrity list like Superman, Wonder Woman or Batman would be. So, I wondered who on Christmas Eve would have been the closest persons to become unlikely heroes. It was the Shepherds. They are the only ones on that night to whom the Angel of the Lord appeared. They were the only ones who saw the heavenly host. Other than witnessing the existence of the Christ Child did God have another mission in mind for them?

This is the story of what may have happened as the shepherds returned to the flocks. The story is not meant to be a prophecy. I did not do any in depth study of the scripture to prove a thesis. It is merely me putting the imagination on paper. I still have the romanticism of a 13-year-old.

Please accept this short Christmas Combat Story.

IN THE FIELDS

"And there were shepherds in the same district living in the fields and keeping watch over their flocks by night."

The Gospel of Luke Chapter 2 Verse 8

"At Christmas, I am always struck by how the spirit of togetherness lies also at the heart of the Christmas story. A young mother and a dutiful father with their baby were joined by poor shepherds and visitors from afar. They came with their gifts to worship the Christ child."

Queen Elizabeth II

It was a cool clear winter night in the hills surrounding Bethlehem. Shepherds in groups of two three or four had combined their sheep into one great flock. They made their camps in a perimeter around the combined herd of sheep. They didn't care if the sheep became mixed together in the morning the sheep knew who their shepherds were, and followed them to new grazing areas.

During the day all the shepherds had been on the lookout for fire wood twigs branches or anything they could burn for warmth. Sometimes all they could do is pull tall dead dry grass and weeds, then they would twist them tightly together to form artificial firewood. They would burn the longest branch from one end to have a ready torch if necessary. They would heat any food they had over these small fires. Sometimes a team of shepherds would acquire some meat a sheep or ram that had died or some animal they had killed while protecting the sheep. Then all the shepherds would share some of their own wood, to build a better fire, and would join in the feast. It was important to finish all the meat because the smell of the leftovers would attract predators. During these ad hoc feasts the shepherds would gather tell stories or pass on news that one of them had heard. By themselves they were a separate clan. Related by profession and comradeship rather than blood.

Tonight, none of the teams had the gift of meat. They were all keeping watch around their small fires. One shepherd was always awake. It was a good system that had lasted hundreds if not thousands of years. The shepherds were talking commenting on how perfect a night it seemed. They were making preparations to start the nights watch protecting the sleeping sheep from predators. There were wolves, wild dogs, jackals, wild boars, bears and even the odd lion. It had been a while since they had actually seen a lion. The best defense for that was to move on, or to quickly build a fence from whatever thorn bushes you could find. Then all the shepherds would form a single unit. A concentrated show of force with the weapons they had the sling and staff and improvised spear from a staff and cherished knife would usually be enough to deter even the larger predators. Whereas wolves hunted in packs, the shepherds defended in numbers enough numbers to deter outright attack. The only defense from more stealthy predators was to be more vigilant. For this the shepherds like their foes had learned to use all their senses. They shepherds could smell the predators. They could differentiate movement of the wind on the grass verses the grass being moved by an animal. The shepherds were sensitive to all the sounds of the day and night and especially the silence.

The shepherds were poor. They had no home and spent all their lives in the fields with the sheep. They were grateful for the bread that the owner of the sheep provided. Sometimes the owner would allow them to roast the sheep or lamb that died of natural causes. None of them had aspirations of anything better. They were a silent brotherhood bonded with the herds. Living to serve, the owners and the sheep.

Three particular shepherds James, John and Luke were one team watching over their sheep in the field. The sheep were the only the responsibility of their employment. They did not own the sheep. The sheep belonged to a well to do person who gained the benefit of the investment. The three shepherds barely earned their daily bread. They were not the best or the brightest nor even the hardest workers. They merely guided the sheep to pasture and water and provided some protection from predators. They were accepted by the sheep as first amongst equals.

James, John and Luke were not well dressed. They wore all they owned and it was still not enough to fight off the winter chill. They had set a fire of what twigs and sticks they could find. The sheep slept close by. warm under their thick wool and content with their Human protectors.

The predators did not like the smell of the fire. It meant Humans and their staffs weapons stones and pack mentality were close by. There were some larger branches kept ready as torches for light and weapons.

James was the eldest. He was in his thirties. He had managed through luck and a good constitution to survive thus far. He could not be considered intelligent but he was wise in his craft. John was James's nephew he was only 20 middle age for the time. Luke was the youngest a not too distant cousin to both James and John he was but 13 just acknowledged as an adult. They were all simple men. None could read. They learned the scriptures by listening as children. They didn't need explanation they were very good at accepting the word as read by their so-called betters.

James's prize possession was his knife. He had found an old dagger that was lost by a soldier in some unnamed battle long ago. James learned to keep it sharp using a river stone worn almost smooth and flat. When any one of the local shepherds needed something cut, they would find James and his razor-edged knife.

John had acquired a yearling tree trunk. It was straight long and hard with a two-inch diameter. John had found a nice rock with the proper coarseness to take off the bark. John smoothed out the wood and knots where the small branches had sprung. Over time the oils from his own hands had given the staff a nice finish and luster.

When Luke was young his mother, a widow, taught him to weave baskets from twigs. One day he had seen a man using a sling to hunt birds. Luke got close enough to get a good look at the sling and observe the hunters form. Luke used fine strips of young tree bark to weave into rope. From there he formed a sling. He spent his young days practicing bringing home the odd bird for his mother to cook. When his mother died, her friends sent Luke to the only relatives they knew, James and John.

The brothers did not begrudge the extra mouth to feed. Luke had some skills like making rustic rope. Luke also brought in birds they could cook. Luke could scare off most predators he saw from a distance with a couple well placed high velocity stones. In short Luke was useful and earned his keep. The brothers treated him like younger brother adopting him into their small clan.

Today Luke had not been lucky with his sling. The three shepherds were around the small fire, eating the last of their bread. There was no need to discuss the order of the watch. John took first watch since he liked to sleep in until dawn. James took the third watch he liked to be up to watch the sun rise. Luke was assigned the middle watch. He would get some sleep and then take. Luke would go back to sleep after waking James. Sometimes Luke would stay awake to keep John company and learn from him. Other times he would not go back to sleep after his watch keeping James company and learning from him. Luke still had the vitality and curiosity of youth.

It had been dark for a while and the night seemed half over. The sky was filled with stars and on this night, there was one star of intense brightness that shone directly, it would seem, over the town of Bethlehem. All of the shepherds wondered what it would be like to live in a house covered from the weather and warm on a bed.

TO SEE WITH YOUR OWN EYES

"And behold, an angel of the Lord stood by them and the glory of God shone around them, and they feared exceedingly"

The Gospel of Luke Chapter 2 Verse 9

The angels taken collectively are called heaven, for they constitute heaven; and yet that which makes heaven in general and in particular is the Divine that goes forth from the Lord and flows into the angels and is received by them.

Emanuel Swedenborg

James John and Luke all mentioned there was no wind. Then the three actually listened for a wind, and that is when they noticed, there were no other sounds, just silence. They heard nothing, no bugs, no animals moving, nothing but perfect quiet. Suddenly, standing over them in front of the fire was an Angel of the Lord. To each of the shepherds the Angel of the Lord appeared exactly as their individual imaginations had pictured Angels when they heard stories as small children. If you asked James John and Luke to describe the Angel, they saw, they would have each given a considerably different account. There was no doubt to each of the Shepherds that this was an Angel. They were terrified.

The Angel of the Lord spoke to them. His voice had an immediate calming effect. The Angel of the Lord told them not be afraid. They should be happy. Their savior, the Christ, arrived. He was born in Bethlehem a town not very far away. You will find him in a manger wearing just swaddling clothes.

Then there was a loud sound as if a giant tree was cracking, or like a thunder and lightning crack but louder and sharper. There was no storm. The sound came from one direction to which the three turned.

Suddenly there appeared Angles. The three all saw the Angels from the exact point of view of their individual imaginations. They would have been amazed and terrified to the point of death such was the glory, might and splendor except that the words of the Angel of the Lord had strengthened their courage.

Then the Angels started singing Glory to God in the highest and on earth peace among men of good will. As rapidly as they had appeared the angels were gone. The shepherds could feel a power they had never known descend upon them. The shepherds understood

THE PILGRIMAGE

"And it came to pass, when the angels had departed from them into heaven, that the shepherds were saying to one another, "Let us go over to Bethlehem and see this thing that has come to pass, which the Lord has made known to us.""

The Gospel of Luke Chapter 2 Verse 15

"A shepherd, in whom the spirit of God works, is more highly esteemed before God than the wisest and most potent in self-wit, without the divine dominion."

Jakob Bohme

James was the first to stand up. He took the torch from the fire. James addressed the other two in a command that was formed like a question/request. "Well I guess we should be going to Bethlehem and see what all this is about." John and Luke didn't need James' statement to convince them. They also had the intention in mind. John and Luke were glad to follow their de facto leader and patriarch of their small clan. John mentioned out loud, "What about the sheep?" They will be fine James replied. They all agreed. Somehow, they knew that if they did what they were prompted to do by the Angel of the Lord their flock would be safe and protected in their absence. The new overwhelming force of will inside of them pushed them forward.

John made sure the fire was out. Luke picked up a small lamb he was caring for. The tiny lamb's mother had died and the rest of the flock had rejected the poor little thing. James was already heading towards the little town and John and Luke followed him.

The sky was extremely bright with stars especially that one star which was apparently directly over the village. This star alone did not move with the passage of the night. The moon was almost full. There was plenty of ambient light to make travel over and through the hills to the town. James kept the torch to fend off any possible attacks they may meet along the way.

As James, john and Luke were walking other shepherds joined them, sometimes in groups sometimes alone. It seemed Brothers and Cousin were the first in line. All the shepherds seemed to follow James deferring to his age. John with his large staff gave James an air of Authority. The shepherds imagined they were following Moses and Aaron. The conversation along the way was the same. Each spoke to the other about the Angels they had seen. No matter that their descriptions differed for there had been many angels in the night sky. The message they heard had no variation, it was exactly the same message at exactly the same time even though they separated in some cases by considerable walking distance. There was not a shred of doubt in a single shepherd's mind that they were on a mission from God.

On their way into town the shepherds felt an air of hostile intent behind them for what was now inside them sensitized them to such things. They could smell the predators in the air. If the shepherds looked behind, they could make out distant shapes on the hills silhouetted against the star filled sky. They did not here the cries of sheep being attacked. The shepherds had faith that their flocks were all safe.

A FORCE TO BE RECKONED WITH

"And when they had seen, they understood what had been told to them concerning this child."

The Gospel of Luke Chapter 2 Verse 17

"The birth of the baby Jesus stands as the most significant event in all history, because it has meant the pouring into a sick world the healing medicine of love which has transformed all manner of hearts for almost two thousand years."

George Matthew Adams

Several formations of shepherds entered the little town of Bethlehem from all directions. They were not dressed in fancy uniforms or carrying terrifying weapons of war. The shepherds were dressed in the poorest of cloth. Many were wearing untanned sheep skins. Only a few had sandals. Some wore head dressings of some sort but most just wore shaggy long hair and beards. The Shepherds did have an ethereal glow about them that gave them a air of power and strength that the best armed and armored warriors did not.

The formations filled the lanes between the buildings that made up the town. People who were out quickly went indoors. The thought was, that there was a peasant revolution and they were here to sack the town. Doors were shut and buttressed. Windows were shuttered. The town was well overcrowded before the arrival of the shepherd army but now it felt abandoned. There was feint lamp light coming from a stable which was almost overpowered by the light of the Star.

The various groups converged on a small stable by an Inn. A ray of light from the mysterious star was shining on the Stable. All the Shepherds knew this was the place

The groups formed orderly lines. There was no fighting or jostling for position. They each felt like they were in a state of Grace. They looked on the tiny pure face of their Savior experiencing nothing but joy and love. They all wished to leave some gift or token. Many of them could only come up with a small whispered blessing that their mothers had taught them. Others left precious little keepsakes that they carried around for ages, pretty rocks that they did not realize were unfinished gem stones. Luke left his little lamb. There was a mother ewe in the stable who had a lamb and she accepted this newcomer.

After seeing the Christ Child, the shepherds reformed into groups in the narrow lanes of the town. The elder shepherds started to converse amongst themselves. They along with others in their group had seen shadows following them from a distance. In their current state of Grace, they were extremely sensitive to the presence of evil. The elder shepherds decided to take their groups out of the city. They needed a place where they could all gather around.

The shepherds left. It took a while for the residents to brave the outdoors again. They did not hear or see what came next in the fields surrounding the little town of Bethlehem.

THE CALM BEFORE THE STORM

"And the shepherds returned, glorifying and praising God for all they had heard and seen, even as it was spoken to them."

The Gospel of Luke Chapter 2 Verse 20

"Grace is a much more accurate word to use when dealing with the state of Human existence. God gives us unmerited favor through Jesus Christ, and since Adam and Eve, our lives have depended on it."

Monica Johnson

The shepherds found a flat open spot. The younger shepherds like Luke were all silent. The oldest of the shepherds like James huddled together and discussed a plan.

James started off. The old dagger he wore in his makeshift belt was like a badge of rank. I know you can all feel it, James stated. Just like when you get the slightest sniff of a predator around your flock. We can all sense the evil approaching. On the way into the village I saw shadows that were not of this world. We need to protect this village as if the people here were our sheep. Most of all we have to protect the Christ Child. I have a plan. We will form a ring around the town and push outward clearing all the evil in our path. We must not let anything get by us. The entire Crowd of shepherds agreed. Each shepherd had the same plan in his head. This was their mission this was their skill set. Now they had divine inspiration. They were lacking nothing.

The shepherds split up into 4 groups made up of three smaller groups of about equal numbers. They surrounded the town each taking point to right left and center of north south east and west. They knew the directions from the stars that still shined brightly in the sky. The small army was enough to circle the entire town several yards apart. As the newly minted soldiers of God looked out towards the hills, they could see the glowing red eyes of their adversaries in the distance.

The shepherds felt no fear, no anxiety only and overwhelming urge to vanquish the evil approaching. They had earthly weapons staves, clubs and slings, but their real weapons were The Grace of God and their Faith.

MUST NOT LET PEACE HAPPEN

"And Jesus asked him, saying, "What is your name?" And he Said "Legion," because many devils had entered into him."

The Gospel of Luke Chapter 8 Verse 30

"Human nature must be changed if we are ever to have an end to war or to correct the wrong situations that make our lives uneasy and our hearts sore. Now Christianity, the power of Jesus Christ, the Holy Spirit of God, is the only force that can change people for good."

Peter Marshall

Nine Months ago, they could sense it. They needed to defile the holy event. They knew they couldn't stop the event but they wanted to destroy the meaning. All the greater Demons in the holy land had been moving back to Israel. Along the way they were picking up lesser Demons and adding them to their force. Earth was their lair that they shared it with the filthy Humans. Compared to them the Humans were mere bugs. The Humans were mortal on this plane. Once they died either killed or by disease, they disappeared forever never to return. Their souls were piling up in the nether world sleeping, waiting for heaven to open. Once heaven was open to their souls, the Humans would become immortal. They would be even to the angels. This was the beginning and it would eventually lead to the Demon's loss of the earthly realm. The Demons knew they could not prevent nor prevail over God. Their wish was to turn God against the Humans. To cause the Humans to behave so outrageously as to forever be cast away from God's Grace as they, the Demons, had been.

The Demons had difficulty moving about the earthly plane in their ethereal form. They needed to possess some living thing in order to move more freely. Humans were difficult as their soul interfered in possession. It wasn't impossible, but you needed to find Human with a significantly soiled, damaged and wounded soul. When you did get in, other Humans took notice and would attempt to cast you out. The attempt usually resulted in the death of the Human that you possessed. Obviously, that necessitated finding a new host to possess. It was a real pain.

Instead the Demons chose to possess living creatures without a soul. For this purpose, they always chose the predators at the top of the food chain. The greater the Demon the greater the predator. Minor Demons possessed the meaner predators and scavengers like the jackal, wild dog, wild boar, or Hyena. The greater Demons reserved the great predators like lions, bears and wolves for themselves. Only the strongest Demons or those lesser demons working in rare cooperation could possess a Human.

The Demon hoard always moved under cover of darkness. They avoided Human habitation. When they rested during the day, they preferred to hideout at the Human burial grounds. There they would pick up more of their own kind.

As they moved closer to the target of their urges, the Demons could feel the pain. For the Demons the Grace of God was an acid, a poison, an electric shock of pain. They had been banished, after the fall, from God's Grace. It was their everlasting punishment. The Demons were once angels who had enjoyed this Grace for eons. Then the Humans arrived. Some angels accepted that God bestowed a Grace on the Humans that the angels had not received. The greatest Angel at the time, Lucifer, had rebelled because of these Humans. The Demons were the angels that backed Lucifer's play. Lucifer lost and they were punished. They were sent to live outside of the Grace of God. Having once known God's Grace, to no longer know it was a constant torture of their own creation.

The greater Demons had to beat and force the lesser Demons to move on and comply. They needed to remove the Grace at its Source otherwise the pain would only continue until the end of times. So, step by step they moved, fighting the torment as they felt the increased Grace of God. They moved towards the ancient land of the Jews, Judah. There in hidden places in the hills surrounding a village they mustered their forces. Daily another greater Demon would arrive driving his lesser Demons in front of him.

The Demons were not a very cooperative bunch but they knew each other from before the fall. They still maintained a certain hierarchy. The stronger of the Demons ruled over the lesser by fear for they too could torment both the living and ethereal.

One night the Demons sensed something great was going to happen. There was a great release of God's Grace. They all howled barked growled and cried in immense pain. Then they saw the heavenly host. They feared. Had God sent his angels to destroy them? They scattered in fear for a while. They spread out around the village. It seemed every Demon for himself.

As quickly as the heavenly host had appeared, they left. The greater Demons gathered the lesser around them. They then very slowly started to move in on the town. The pain of the Grace was intense but now they were sure of the location and Source. The Source of God's Grace on earth was no longer moving. The Grace was here.

The Demons with their predator eyes could see in the distance a rag tag group of Humans. They felt an aura of God's Grace on theses Humans that was barely perceptible over the power of that one Source. It seemed to the greater Demons that these Humans were forming for battle. they were establishing a defensive perimeter.

Now those Humans having formed a circle around the town started to move forward inviting battle. The greatest of the Demons roared. He had possessed a Lion. The other greater Demons answered with roars and howls of their own. They pushed the lesser Demons forward to crush these puny Humans.

THE BATTLE IS JOINED

"Then having summoned the twelve apostles, he gave them power and authority over all the devils, and to cure diseases."
The Gospel of Luke Chapter 9 Verse 1

"Now the seventy-two returned with joy, saying lord even the devils are subject to us in your name. But he said to them, "I was watching Satan fall as lightning from heaven. Behold, I have given you power to tread upon serpents and scorpions, and over all the might of the enemy; and nothing shall hurt you. But do not rejoice in this, that the spirits are subject to you; rejoice rather in this, that your names are written in heaven.""
The Gospel of Luke Chapter 10 Verses 17 to 20

"The story of everyday people rising up to fight against evil to protect their families - it's a story that we've seen play out throughout history and across the world today."
Matthew Heineman

James saw the red eyes in the distance. When he felt all the shepherds were in place and ready, James shouted Yahweh! and took a step forward. All the shepherds followed James' lead. They were slow and deliberate. There wasn't a panicked charge. Each shepherd could make out the red eyes, reflecting the ambient light, of the force coming towards them.

Luke had picked up a collection of perfect sling stones that he always carried in a pouch connected to his belt. When he met other young shepherds in the field, he showed them how to make the rustic rope of which the sling was composed. Each time Luke helped another Young Shepherd make a sling his method was improved and the resulting sling even better than the previous. Luke enjoyed the competition of target practice and although his sling wasn't as good as the newer ones, he constructed, Luke was an expert with it. All the young shepherds imagined themselves the next King David looking for their Goliath.

The Shepherds having been given the understanding of the situation by God's Grace now knew that they were defending the next King David. As if on order all the young shepherds with slings unleashed a volley fire of missiles radiating out in all directions from the circle they formed around the little town. Each and every missile found its mark and dispatched a foe from the fight, but there were many foes. Several more times they loaded their slings and sent unerring missiles into the onslaught before the remaining Demons had closed the distance.

The lesser Demons were running like mad at the defenders of the town. They had used abused tortured and disfigured the animals that they possessed. Now the Demons charged with wild abandon. They did not care what happened to these earthly bodies. Suddenly some of the Demons were struck with missiles. They didn't care about that because even seriously wounded they would force the poor creatures to fight to the last. However; these missiles had an ethereal power. They had been touched by someone who had come near to touching the Source. This the lesser Demons could not tolerate. The pain forced them from their tormented captives. They left the animals bodies with a shriek and were banished into the void. The animals fell, exhausted near death but not dead. They would all slowly recover and attempt to make it back to where they had been captured. One or two of the lesser Demons seeing the slaughter of the others and being far enough from the Greater Demons forcing them to the slaughter abandoned the battle and ran away into the wilderness. But there were a great multitude of demons and the survivors closed the distance until they were too close for the slings and missiles to be used against them.

The Demons came right at the picket line of shepherds. The intent of the Demons was to cause a fear and panic in these Humans and send them screaming into the town. There they would cause additional fear and panic to the Towns Folk. The Demons themselves were not strong enough to harm the Source. They knew the prophecy, Psalm 34 Verse 20 "He keeps all his bones, not one of them is broken." The Demons could not defeat the Source but they could initiate the cause of injury to those around the Source. Maybe just maybe, the Source would withdraw His Grace from these Humans and leave them ever under the dominion of the fallen.

Now the Shepherds with staves and clubs joined the fight. Each shepherd waved a mighty swing as if they were fighting off a wolf from attacking the flock. Every time one of their staves or clubs struck home that Demon was thrown from his host and the host laid prone.

The greater more powerful Demons, seeing the confusion in the melee, felt that the thin line of shepherds was ready to break. The Demons moved forward Lions Wolves Bears and great Boars. Unlike the lesser Demons they did not move forward with a wild run. That was beyond the dignity of their rank. The greater the Demon the more they felt the pain of the Grace. They walked slow and determined with hubris and disrespect for their Human foe.

A few of the younger shepherds now saw their Goliaths coming. Those that could, unleashed a powerful onslaught of missiles. The hosts of the greater Demons were struck multiple times. They did not seem to stop but advanced constantly forward.

The Greater Demons felt the pain of the missiles. Their hosts bodies were large enough to absorb the injury. The Demons' malevolence was strong enough to absorb the pain of the Grace. They let out a roar or howl and continued onward.

Luke was looking around for a club to defend himself when a Jackal jumped straight at him. Luke caught the small predator. Luke could feel the malevolence hidden in the creature. Luke had always had a love of animals. He hunted out of necessity. He never killed for sport. Luke was at one with nature and knew God had created all the creatures and each served a purpose. He felt compassion for all living things.

Even before receiving the Grace, Luke had a near-pure soul. He never showed jealousy and rarely anger. Luke freely gave of everything he had and joyfully received.

Like two opposite poles of a magnet attracting each other, Luke found his Grace enhanced soul was able to pull the malevolent spirits out of the animals and hold them prisoner in himself. He fell back out of the immediate fight. Luke knew his mission now was to intercept any Demon that made it past the line of defense.

With every bit of sentience, the poor creatures had left, they rebelled against their captors. They were strengthened by the presence of God's Grace while their Demon captors were weakened. The creatures sensed their freedom laid within Luke. Any Demon who made it through the line found himself being carried towards the young shepherd. They tried to fight and make the animal turn away but their captives were using the last of their strength and would not be denied.

Time and time again Luke caught a creature and pulled the malevolent spirit from it. The creature would then run away from the town and the battle. The Demons would scream they were now the captives and they were being tormented by the presence of Luke's near-pure and Grace enhanced soul. The Demons started fighting to escape. Luke now had many Demons inside of himself. He knew he had to get the malevolence away from the Source. Luke ran off into the wilderness away from everyone and everything.

While Luke was gathering up those Demons the battle at the line had hit critical mass. A few of minor Demons were being swept up when the greater Demons attack hit the defenders. There were not so many of these Large Predators but they were fearsome. Every shepherd swarmed on the greater Demon/predator closest to himself.

The Demons were caught off guard. Their arrogance hadn't accounted for a determined attack from a fearless foe. They, the Demons, were being beaten from all around they could not defend themselves. Even the poor predator hosts were fighting against the Demons, determined to escape their captivity.

The Demons could feel the strength of their hosts dwindling. They looked for a way out. The Demons searched for a tainted wounded dirty soul to possess. Surely one of these violent men was less than worthy of God's Grace.

Suddenly the Demons felt themselves being pulled away from their hosts and into one of the Humans. They were confused. This did not ever happen. They, the formerly fiercest force on earth, were being captured and held captive. Fear and panic were feelings they had not experienced since the fall. Now the Demons were confused and lashed out inside their Human captors.

The shepherds with the purest souls knew what to do. As soon as they grappled with the possessed predator, they could feel its agony. At the same time the shepherds could feel the fear of the Demon. The shepherds seized and captured the demon spirit. Like Luke they knew they had to get this malevolent force far away from the Source. As each demon was captured another shepherd host/prison guard fled into the wilderness.

It was a miracle that none of the possessed animals had been killed by the shepherds. Some were wounded some were dazed all were exhausted. As they were freed from their captors by the Grace of God, they moved out of the area. The only evidence they left behind was some blood trails, foot prints and the occasional bruise or cut on a shepherd. Time and the wind cleared all of these.

The shepherds were in a state of Grace and did not hunt down the wounded predators. They understood that God's creatures were not willing participants in the battle. The remaining shepherds were concerned about their younger brethren. Should they go and search them out or should they return to their flocks. They sensed their battle was over. They also under stood that their brothers had made a decision to sacrifice themselves. The shepherds knew their bothers were still fighting and it was a fight the captor shepherds needed to win alone.

The remaining shepherds went back to their flocks. For a long time, they were not bothered by any predators seeking to carry off a lamb sheep ram or goat. They praised the Glory of God. They did not brag about their accomplishments for they knew it was all God's Grace. The shepherds rejoiced because they understood and knew that their names were written in heaven. None of the older shepherds lived to see the Source enter His ministry. The next time they met the Source, was when the gates to the kingdom were opened. The Source allowed them place towards the front of the line.

EPILOGUE

"One day Jesus called together his twelve disciples and gave them power and authority to cast out all Demons and to heal all diseases. Then he sent them out to tell everyone about the Kingdom of God and to heal the sick."

The Gospel of Luke Chapter 9 Verses 1 and 2

"The scripture is filled with examples of genuine masculinity; you could mine David's story for probably a year by itself. And we have to get the masculinity of Jesus back. Not the pale-faced altar boy, but the man that made a weapon and cleared the temple, who boldly cast out Demons and calmed the raging sea."

John Eldredge

They sensed it 30 years later the former shepherds sensed it. The Source, The Lord, the Messiah, the Christ they had protected long ago, was coming into his ministry and Glory. After the young shepherds of near-pure heart had captured the Demons within themselves, they fled into the wilderness keeping the dangerous spirits away from their fellow man. There in the desert, mountains and hills the shepherds were tormented by the Demons who were trying to get free in order to possess a dark tainted impure soul. The Demons forced the shepherds to survive by eating and drinking mean and impure things. The shepherds became scarred, emaciated, filthy and nearly naked. They looked more like walking corpses than living men. The shepherds still had the strength of their near-pure souls enhanced by the Grace of God and now they had hope.

Slowly, they moved in the direction of the Source. The Demons fought bitterly against any progress because just like before, 30 years ago, the closer to the Source the more pain the Demons felt and the weaker they became. The shepherds still kept their distance from civilization first because people would force them away afraid of what they were and secondly because the shepherds were not going to risk the death that would set their captives free.

The shepherds wanted to find the Source. The Source, for now having entered his ministry would destroy their tormentors. The Demons knew that banishment was near. Their mission had failed. When finally, the poor shepherds came close to their goal they would shout with whatever strength they had left. "Jesus, forgive me a sinner!" For they knew that all have fallen short of the Grace of God. They knew that the Grace would again be bestowed upon them for all you need is ask. sometimes it was the Demons who were able to scream first. They knew the truth they sought to destroy faith they announced that Jesus was the Savior. The Demons knew that the ignorant were looking for someone politically economically or militarily powerful. If they proclaimed Jesus as the Source the people would expect more than the Word. The demons were silenced and banished

In the end the result was the same. Jesus would free the shepherds from their burden and the Demons would be banished into the void.

The shepherds would follow Jesus. they would meet some other shepherds who over 30 years ago had also sacrificed themselves proving God's plan that with his Grace the Humans were as strong and worthy as all his other creations.

The Source found Luke near a lake in a graveyard where he banished all the Demons Luke held prisoner.

Nothing is free in this world except for the Grace of God.

ABOUT THE AUTHOR

Michael F. Tuman is a Fourth Degree Knight of Columbus, who Joined the fraternal organization in 2007 during one of his military tours in Afghanistan

Mike Tuman (Flying Monkey Five November) (Psyopguru) (Two Gun Tuman) served 27 years as a Chicago Police Detective with assignments ranging from Auto Theft, Homicide and Special Victims Unit. He also lasted 37 Years in the United States Army Reserve rising to the illustrious and rare rank of CW5 Chief Warrant Officer 5. He is a two-time graduate of the Defense Language Institute Foreign Language Center at the Presidio of Monterey California and the Presidio of San Francisco California. He deployed overseas five times in the service of his Country.

Mike can be contacted at:

https://www.facebook.com/mike.tuman.353
https://twitter.com/FlyingM01110187
https://www.linkedin.com/in/michael-tuman-b9418715
https://www.pinterest.com/flyingmonke
https://www.youtube.com/channel/UCtlgIQflmelaiccUjW6s_FA
https://www.reddit.com/user/flyingmonkey5nov
www.flyingmonkey5november@gmail.com